for my editor

ACKNOWLEDGMENTS
Thanks as always to Cecilia Yung, Annie Ericsson and
Sara Kreger, for helping me make this book look so good.
Also thanks to the people and mountains of Peru for
reminding me how big and exciting the world can be.

NANCY PAULSEN BOOKS
A division of Penguin Young Readers Group.
Published by The Penguin Group.
Penguin Group (USA) Inc.,
375 Hudson Street, New York, NY 10014, U.S.A.
Penguin Group (Canada), 90 Eglinton Avenue East, Suite 700, Toronto,
Ontario M4P 2Y3, Canada (a division of Pearson Penguin Canada Inc.).
Penguin Books Ltd, 80 Strand, London WC2R 0RL, England.
Penguin Ireland, 25 St. Stephen's Green, Dublin 2, Ireland
(a division of Penguin Books Ltd.).
Penguin Group (Australia), 250 Camberwell Road, Camberwell,
Victoria 3124, Australia (a division of Pearson Australia Group Pty Ltd).
Penguin Books India Pvt Ltd, 11 Community Centre,
Panchsheel Park, New Delhi - 110 017, India.
Penguin Group (NZ), 67 Apollo Drive, Rosedale, Auckland 0632, New Zealand
(a division of Pearson New Zealand Ltd).
Penguin Books (South Africa) (Pty) Ltd, 24 Sturdee Avenue,
Rosebank, Johannesburg 2196, South Africa.
Penguin Books Ltd, Registered Offices: 80 Strand, London WC2R 0RL, England.

Design by Annie Ericsson. Text set in Egyptienne.
The art was done with acrylics and black pencil on vellum.
Library of Congress Cataloging-in-Publication Data
is available upon request.
ISBN 978-0-399-25636-3

1 3 5 7 9 10 8 6 4 2

DAVE HOROWITZ

CHICO
THE BRAVE

Nancy Paulsen Books 🌀 An Imprint of Penguin Group (USA) Inc.

ONCE UPON A TIME,

in the mountains of Peru, a chick was born who was afraid of everything.

And when I say he was afraid of everything—

I mean he was afraid of *everything*.

HELP! I'm being followed...

This poor little guy was even afraid
of his own shadow.

One day, the chick's father decided something must be done. "Chico," he said, "have I ever told you the story of the Golden Chicken?"

"I don't think so," said the chick. "It sounds scary."

"Not at all," said his father. "The Golden Chicken is a good guy—a *superbird*. Whenever there's trouble, he, um, swoops down from those there mountains like lightning and saves the day."

"*Re-e-e-eally?*" said the chick.

"Yes, really. . . . Now, why don't you go outside and play?"

Chico went outside, but the world was just as scary as ever.

"Boy," he said to himself, "being a chicken stinks. I wonder what makes the Golden Chicken so brave."

And then he had an idea . . .

"I'll go ask him myself!"

So Chico packed himself a lunch and went
out looking for the legendary bird.

He walked and walked, and soon found himself surrounded by llamas. "Excuse me," he said. "Have any of you guys seen the Golden Chicken?"

"The golden *what?*" They all laughed.

"The Golden Chicken," said Chico from behind his sandwich. "My dad says he's a superbird who lives in these mountains. Whenever there's trouble, he swoops down like lightning and saves the day."

"Oh, *that* Golden Chicken," said one of the llamas. "Why didn't you say so? Of course we know him—he's a very good friend of ours. In fact, he lives on top of that mountain right there."

The llama pointed to the tallest, scariest mountain the chick had ever seen.

"Oh, well," said Chico. "Once I find that Golden Chicken, I'll never be scared again."

And so the chick began to climb . . .

And climb.

And climb.

And climb.

He climbed until there was no more mountain
to climb. But there was no Golden Chicken up
there. There was no nothing! There was only sky.

Suddenly a mighty wind rose up and blew the
chick right off the mountain and into thin air . . .

And across the sky . . .

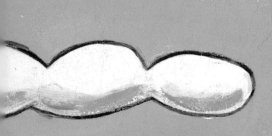

. . . where he got an idea.

Chico threw his wings wide and let
the winds carry him. Before he knew
it, the kid was soaring.

BUT MEANWHILE . . .

Back at home, there was real trouble.
Remember those llamas from a few pages
ago? Well, turns out they were the dreaded
Llama Llama Gang from Cashapampa and
they were turning the town upside down!

Just then, a shadow shot across the sky like
lightning. "Uh-oh," said one of the llamas.
"You think that's the Golden Chicken the kid
was talking about?"

"I don't know," said another llama, "but
let's not stick around to find out."

And those terrible llamas were never seen
again. But come to think of it, neither was
our frightened little chick.

For in the mountains of Peru there was
a hero born that day, and they call him
Chico the Brave.